Be Careful, it's a Hippo!

Written by Alice Russ Watson

Illustrated by Emma Nyari

Collins

Who and what is in this story?

Listen and say

Download the audio at www.collins.co.uk/839714

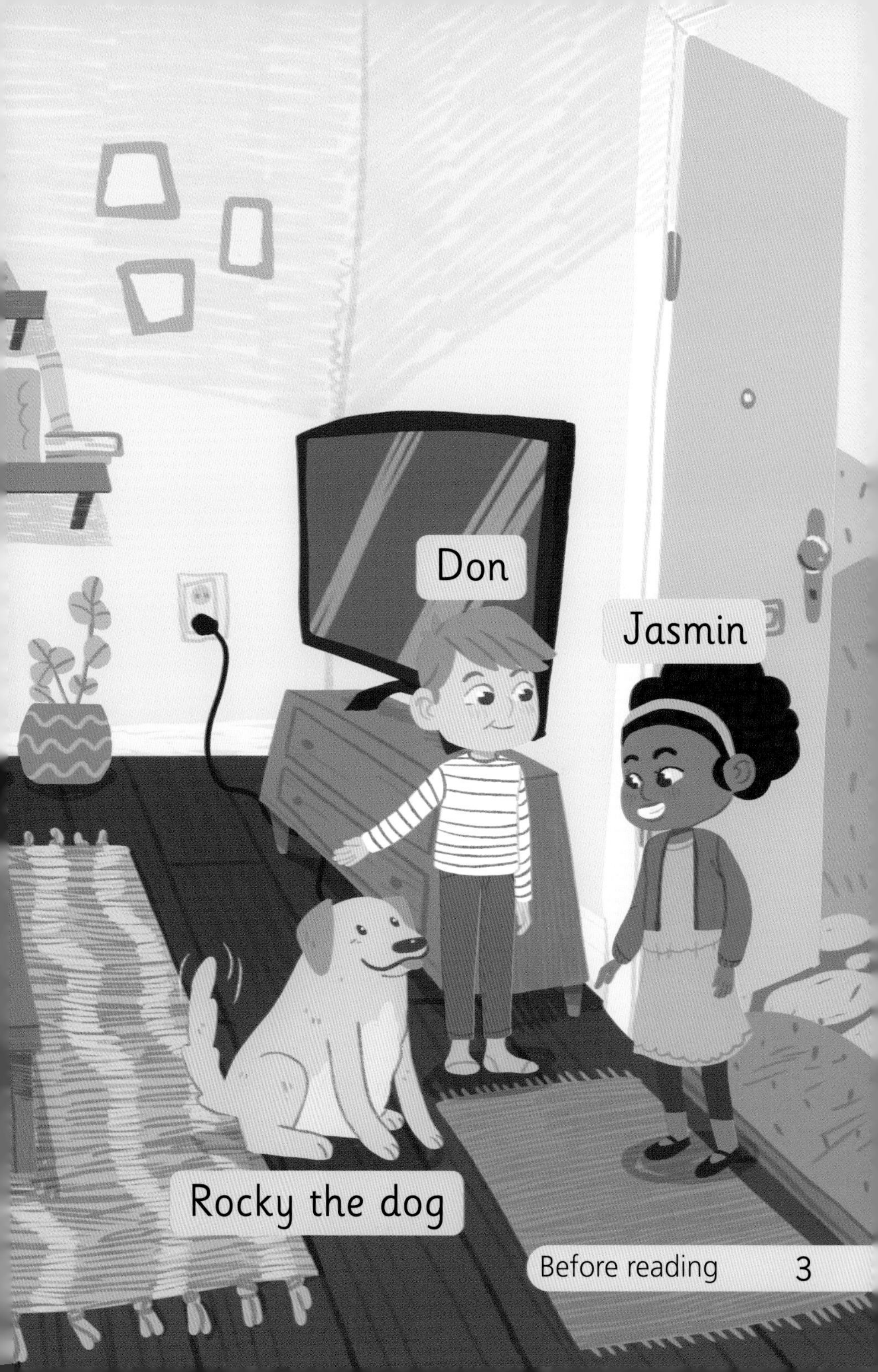
Don
Jasmin
Rocky the dog

Don and Jasmin were at Don's house.

"Let's watch TV," Don said.

But Jasmin wanted to play.

"I have a better idea," she said, and she sat on the table.

"Why are you sitting on the table?" asked Don.

"It's not a table. It's a boat," said Jasmin.

Don sat next to Jasmin and looked at her.

She was pointing at the rug.

"Look at the fish in the river!" she said.

Don looked but he only saw the rug.

"Look at the forest!" said Jasmin. "Look at the birds!"

Don looked, but he only saw the plants and the books.

7

"Be careful! It's a hippo!" said Jasmin.

"That's not a hippo, that's Rocky!"
said Don.

"This forest is beautiful," Jasmin said.
"What can you see, Don?"

Don looked again. He started to see
the forest.

He could see the river, the fish and the birds. He could see lots of things.

"I can see a snake," he said, "and a duck! And I can see ..."

"... A CROCODILE!"

"Oh no!" said Jasmin. "Quick! Let's go!"

"No!" said Don. "Let's help the duck. The crocodile wants to eat it."

"That is difficult," said Jasmin.
"Crocodiles are fast."

"What can we do?" asked Don.

12

"Give me some fruit," said Jasmin.

Don gave Jasmin an orange.

She threw it at the crocodile!

The orange hit the crocodile on the head and the duck was safe.

Now it's quiet by the river.

Don and Jasmin are happy.

But, oh no!

"Be careful! It's the hippo!" said Don.

"He's very angry," said Jasmin.
"What can we do?"

"Don't worry," said Don.
"I've got an idea."

"He isn't angry. He's hungry!"
Don gave the hippo some cookies.
The hippo liked cookies and he ate
them all.

"You're very clever," said Jasmin.
"You're clever, too!" said Don.

"I'm tired. Let's stop the boat now,"
said Jasmin.

"OK," said Don and he stood up.

But, oh no!

They fell in the river!

"What now?" said Jasmin.

"Don't worry!" said Don.
"The hippo can help us."

"That was fun," said Jasmin.

"What a good hippo you are, Rocky," said Don to his dog. "Do you like the forest?"

Picture dictionary

Listen and repeat

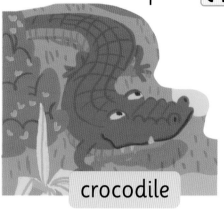

crocodile

duck

forest

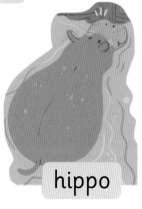

hippo

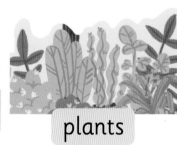

plants

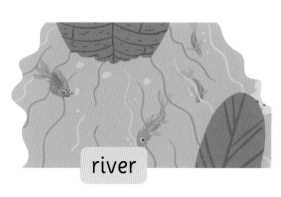

river

snake

1 Look and order the story

2 Listen and say

Collins

Published by Collins
An imprint of HarperCollins*Publishers*
Westerhill Road
Bishopbriggs
Glasgow
G64 2QT

HarperCollins*Publishers*
1st Floor, Watermarque Building
Ringsend Road
Dublin 4
Ireland

William Collins' dream of knowledge for all began with the publication of his first book in 1819.

A self-educated mill worker, he not only enriched millions of lives, but also founded a flourishing publishing house. Today, staying true to this spirit, Collins books are packed with inspiration, innovation and practical expertise. They place you at the centre of a world of possibility and give you exactly what you need to explore it.

© HarperCollins*Publishers* Limited 2020

10 9 8 7 6 5 4 3 2

ISBN 978-0-00-839714-2

Collins® and COBUILD® are registered trademarks of HarperCollins*Publishers* Limited

www.collins.co.uk/elt

British Library Cataloguing in Publication Data

A catalogue record for this publication is available from the British Library.

Author: Alice Russ Watson
Illustrator: Emma Nyari (Beehive)
Series editor: Rebecca Adlard
Commissioning editor: Zoë Clarke
Publishing manager: Lisa Todd
Product managers: Jennifer Hall and Caroline Green
In-house editor: Alma Puts Keren
Project manager: Emily Hooton
Editor: Frances Amrani
Proofreaders: Natalie Murray and Michael Lamb
Cover designer: Kevin Robbins
Typesetter: 2Hoots Publishing Services Ltd
Audio produced by id audio, London
Reading guide author: Emma Wilkinson
Production controller: Rachel Weaver
Printed and bound by: GPS Group, Slovenia

Download the audio for this book and a reading guide for parents and teachers at www.collins.co.uk/839714